MW01490089

MORE
INCREDIBLE
TRUE
ADVENTURES

Don L. Wulffson

MORE INCREDIBLE TRUE ADVENTURES

Illustrated with photographs

COBBLEHILL BOOKS

Dutton   New York

For Pam

PICTURE CREDITS

Copyright, New York *Daily News*, 80, 87; Copyright, Funk & Wagnalls Publishing Company, 44, 49; Montgomery County Historical Society, Dayton, Ohio, 31, 33, 40; P. Paisley, 64, 67, 69; Leonard Lee Rue III, 55; Copyright, Matthew Thayer, 14; United Nations Refugee Relief (UNHCR), 101 (K. Gaugler), 107 (R. Manin); U.S. Air Force Academy, 90, 95; U.S. Army, 19 (Pfc. N. F. Buchman), 21 (SP5 Robert C. Lafoon), 28 (Staff Sgt. Robert R. Ellis); U.S. Navy, 103 (PH1/AC R. H. Green).

"Attacked by a Grizzley," adapted from the story by Gordon Carlson, courtesy of *Read Magazine*, © copyright 1978, Field Publications.

Every effort has been made to contact the copyright holders of the photographs used for "Jungle of Death" and "The *Castle* Sinking."

Library of Congress Cataloging-in-Publication Data
Wulffson, Don L.
  More incredible true adventures.
  Includes index.
  Summary: Nine true adventure stories include the experiences of passengers when their airplane's roof comes off, patrons trapped in a library during a flood, and explorers pursued by cannibals.
  1. Adventure and adventures—Juvenile literature. [1. Adventure and adventurers] I. Title.
G525.W96 1989   904   89-1531
ISBN 0-525-65000-8

Published in the United States by E.P. Dutton,
New York, N. Y., a division of Penguin Books USA Inc.
Published simultaneously in Canada by
Fitzhenry & Whiteside Limited, Toronto

Printed in the United States of America
First Edition   10 9 8 7 6 5 4 3 2 1

CONTENTS

1

THIRTEEN MINUTES OF TERROR

It was the afternoon of April 29, 1988. In Hilo, Hawaii, ninety passengers had settled in their seats aboard Aloha Airlines flight 243. The plane moved into position for takeoff. The engines whined, shrieked. The jetliner rocketed down the runway and lifted off into the air. It climbed higher and higher. At 24,000 feet it leveled off, high above the blue waters of Hawaii.

The flight was to have been a short "hop" from one island to another, from Hilo to Honolulu. It never made it. Forty-five minutes, that's how long the flight was to have taken. Instead, just thirteen minutes later, it was over.

Businessman Jim Kilgariff had chosen a window seat. "The plane had just taken off," he said. "I was just relaxing. I was thinking of taking a nap. Suddenly I heard a blast. It was a huge *whoompf* sound. Then there was a powerful rush of air. Yellow oxygen masks dropped down, but they were ripped away by the wind. Tons of trash came flying at me. At first I had my hands over my face. Then I managed to look around. All I could see was sky! The roof of the plane had come off!"

Said another passenger. "I had a book in one hand and a calculator in the other. Then there was this explosion, and suddenly my hands were empty. The calculator and book had disappeared into thin air. A monster wind raced through the plane. Plastic cups, luggage, and pieces of the plane blasted through everything like a tornado. Some people had their shoes and some of their clothing sucked right off of them. Most of the plane around me was gone. I was sure a bomb had gone off."

The explosion, it was learned later, was not caused by a bomb. There was a weakness in the metal roof of the plane. It cracked. And then the pressure inside the cabin blew away part of the plane. About a third of the metal sides and roof were gone. The hole went from behind the cockpit back to where the wings began.

Right before the blast, passenger Bill Flannigan was talking with his wife, Joy. "A stewardess," said Mr. Flannigan, "was serving soft drinks. She asked my wife and me if we'd like a soda. She was handing my wife a glass. Suddenly the glass disappeared. Then the stewardess disappeared! She just flew right out of the top of the plane!"

Flannigan continued: "Just like that the plane was wide open. The roof and sides were gone. The passengers were strapped to their seats. It was like riding in a convertible. Only there were dozens of people in the seats. And we were five miles up in the air!"

"It was our seat belts," said a lady from Ohio. "That's what saved us. Everyone had his seat belt on. At first I didn't think they would hold us. But they seemed okay. But then the floor started to buckle and bend. I thought it would come apart. I was sure the seats would rip right out of the floor. I thought that, strapped in our seats, we'd fly right out into space. It would be like what happened to that poor stewardess. I kept thinking about her. I felt so badly for her. She was a very nice girl."

Another stewardess almost met the same fate. "She was crawling down the aisle," said Dan Dennin. "She almost got sucked out. Pillows and carry-on bags and everything else was getting sucked out. But she hung on. A couple of people in aisle seats were holding on to her."

Most of the passengers said how calm and cool everyone was. Most had been injured by pieces of flying glass and metal.

Others had been burned when live electrical wires rained down on them when the ceiling came apart. Everyone was terribly shocked and frightened. Still, no one panicked. People did their best to try to help each other.

Said passenger David Jackson: "There was no more airplane around us. We were like a bunch of people flying on a carpet of metal. It was really weird and terrifying. We were scared, and a lot of people were hurt. Still, we all tried to hang together. The woman next to me had a window seat. There was really nothing between her and death. There was nothing between her and a drop of thousands of feet. But she was brave. I held on to her and she held on to me. We kept each other as calm as we could."

Many passengers put on life jackets. Below, all that could be seen was blue-green water. Word had spread that they were going to make a crash landing in the ocean.

Sylvia Hudson, of Oregon, was sitting

back farther in the plane, away from the gaping hole. She described what she saw and what was going through her mind: "We were going down. Everyone was sure we were going into the ocean. Ahead of me all I could see were all these people riding in an open-air airplane. And they— and all of us—were going into the drink. I figured the pilot was going to make some sort of a landing on the water.

"Then a terrible thought started going through my head. I wondered about the pilot. I thought he might be dead. From where I was sitting, all I could see in front of me was the people and the wreckage. I didn't think we had a pilot anymore."

Fortunately, she was wrong. The plane still had its pilot. A very good one. His name was Robert Schornstheimer. He was known for his strong nerves and steady hand.

"I didn't know what had happened exactly, not at first," said the pilot. "But all of a sudden there was this horrible noise behind me. The plane was flying funny. It was pitching back and forth, and there was a big drag on it. At first I thought of turning around and heading back to Hilo. But at this point we were closer to the island of Maui. I contacted the airport on Maui. I told them we had an emergency and we were coming in."

"I give credit to the pilot," said John Lopez, another passenger. "He brought the plane down so smoothly. It was just like riding in a Cadillac."

"Most of us didn't even know we were coming in for a landing," said a woman seated near Lopez. "We had our heads down and our hands behind our necks. I peeked out. That's when I saw the runway. My heart pounded. I was scared the plane was going to break in half when it landed. But it didn't. I was amazed it didn't fall apart and explode when it hit the runway."

At Maui airport, people on the ground stared in wonder as the plane came in.

The battered Aloha Airlines jetliner after landing in Maui, Hawaii

Steven Songstad, a lawyer, was on his way to catch a plane when he saw the shattered jet approach the runway. "I was just pulling into the parking lot at the airport," he said. "I saw it coming in. At first I thought it was just a lousy paint job. And then I realized it was a huge gaping hole."

"I couldn't believe what I was seeing,"

added a worker at the airport. "I dropped to my knees in disbelief. It was just like a normal landing, only you could see all these people sitting in their seats. It was the craziest thing I've ever seen. The plane wobbled a little as it came in, but it landed just fine. The guy at the controls must have been one terrific pilot."

Pilot Schornstheimer taxied the plane to a stop. Ground crews came running. Ambulances and fire trucks rushed to the scene.

People in the rear of the plane made their way to exits. One by one they slid down emergency chutes.

The passengers in the ripped open front of the plane were in shock. They just sat in their seats. They looked around. They couldn't believe they were on the ground. They couldn't believe it was over.

Members of the emergency crews were all around the plane. Some climbed aboard and pushed through the wreckage. They yelled at the people. They told them they would be okay, that they were safe.

No one seemed to hear. The people acted as though they were deaf. Blank eyes stared. No one moved for a long while. Then finally the silence was broken. A young man slowly unbuckled his seat belt. He stood up. He looked at the ground crews. Then he looked at the other passengers. "We're alive!" he said in a loud but shaky voice. "It's not possible. It's not. But we made it. We're alive!"

2

TUNNELS OF FEAR

The year was 1968. The place: Cu Chi, Vietnam. A bloody war was raging.

Private First Class Mike Lang leaned against a wrecked tank. Somewhere deep in the jungle a machine gun rattled deadly fire. Overhead a U.S. helicopter gunship streaked in low, toward the action. Mike watched as it fired two air-to-ground missiles. They exploded with a cracking *whoompf* sound. Red flames and black smoke billowed up from a green hillside.

Mike shifted his gaze. A few yards away Lieutenant Knowles and Sergeant Art

Reno crouched around the entrance to a Viet Cong tunnel. The two men talked in hushed tones. Reno looked knowingly at Mike for a moment. Then he lowered himself into the shaft leading down to the tunnel.

Mike felt empty, ashamed. He should be going down into the tunnel with Reno. But he couldn't. He didn't have the courage. At least in his own mind, he had become the one thing he thought he could never be: a coward.

It was not the enemy that scared him. It was not the fighting. Being wounded or killed, that really wasn't it either. It was the tunnels—and the crawling terror that might be in them. That's what terrified him. Never again would he go down into the tunnels of Cu Chi.

His first day in Vietnam, over five months before, Mike had learned about the tunnels. Below Cu Chi, the Viet Cong had dug miles of them. They had built a whole world of their own down there.

Entering a Viet Cong tunnel

Most of the tunnels were only two or three feet high and about as wide. They zigzagged. They branched out in every direction. And every now and then there were trapdoors. Some of these led to the surface. Others led down to other, still lower tunnels.

The tunnels served the Viet Cong in

many ways. Unseen, they could travel long distances. Then they would crawl out of the tunnels and attack American bases. When the Americans came after them, they would disappear back underground.

Many of the tunnels led to room-size compartments. Some of these were used by the Viet Cong for eating and sleeping. Others were used for storing food and weapons. The biggest and best were actually underground hospitals. In them, trained doctors and nurses took care of wounded soldiers.

The Americans had tried every way possible to destroy the tunnels and the Viet Cong in them. They had tried blowing them up. They had tried tear gas. They had even tried flooding them with river water.

But none of these things had worked. The only way to fight the Viet Cong in the tunnels was to go down after them. The battle had to be fought hand-to-hand, down in the filth and blackness of the

A "tunnel rat" inside a Viet Cong tunnel

tunnels. It was an especially ugly and frightening place in which to take on the enemy.

Not many men wanted to fight in the tunnels. But Mike Lang did. His sixth day in Vietnam he volunteered to fight underground. He became what was known as a "tunnel rat."

In the months that followed, Mike had faced every danger possible in the tunnels. In the blackness, there were Viet Cong soldiers. There were booby traps of every kind, usually bombs that were set off by the touch of a single tiny wire. There were ants, spiders, rats, bugs.

There were also snakes.

And it was a snake that had turned Mike into a coward. He had been headed out of a tunnel two days ago. Suddenly his head touched something like a big salami. He reached up to push it away. It slithered onto him and began coiling around him. It was a huge snake! He stabbed at it with his knife as it wound tighter and tighter. Screaming, Mike had backed out of the hole. He was still screaming as men killed the snake and pulled it off of him. It turned out to be a python. It measured almost seven feet in length.

And now all Mike could do was sit and watch while others fought. He could only sit and stare at the hole Reno had entered.

"Tunnel rats" almost always worked in pairs. But Mike was a coward. He had let his friend Reno go down alone.

Lieutenant Knowles walked over to Mike. "I know what you're goin' through," said Knowles. He forced a smile. "A man can only go down into that hell so many times. Then he reaches a breaking point. I've seen it happen a hundred times. Nothin' to be ashamed of. You've done your bit, and enough's enough. Dang, after what you been through it's . . ."

The officer's words were cut off by a muffled bang underground. Then there was the sound of gunfire from down in the tunnel. Knowles raced to the two-way radio propped near the entrance to the tunnel. "Reno, you hit?" he demanded. "Reno, come in. Come in. You hit?"

The radio crackled briefly. "Yeah," rasped Reno's voice.

Mike would say later that he can't really remember deciding to go into the tunnel after his friend. He said he remembers those moments as though he was sleep-walking. It was as though he was waking up from one nightmare and stepping into another one.

Whispering Reno's name, he found himself slithering down a vertical shaft. Then he let himself drop. He was in the tunnel. On hands and knees he began to crawl forward. In one hand he had a pistol. In the other a flashlight.

The tunnel stank, and it was very narrow. The roots of trees brushed against his back as he crawled through the dark. He shined his light on the thick, twisted roots. They looked like snakes. Hundreds of them seemed to be everywhere above and around him.

He continued on. To his left was a small room dug into the side of the tunnel. He aimed his flashlight into it. The roof was covered with mosquitoes and other insects. The floor of the underground room was strewn with rotten, stinking rice. Huge rats crawled through the stuff, eating it.

Mike turned his flashlight ahead. He heard a moan. It was Art Reno.

"Mike?" asked Reno.

"Hang in there, man," said Mike. "Hang on."

Suddenly the floor between Mike and Reno moved a bit. It was a trapdoor. It lifted up. For an instant Mike could see the eyes of the Viet Cong. The barrel of an automatic rifle appeared. Mike fired his pistol twice. There was the sound of wood splintering and a yelp of pain. The trapdoor closed.

Mike crab-walked down the tunnel. He came to the trapdoor. He fired his pistol straight down through it. Then he made his way to Art Reno. "I'm gonna get you out, man. I'll get you out," said Mike.

Reno had been wounded in the face and both legs. "Thanks, man." he said. "That lousy little creep back there got the drop on me. Watch out for him. He's still down here somewhere."

Mike tied Art's wrists together. Then

he looped the man's arms about his neck. He began crawling backwards, down the tunnel, dragging his friend. He passed over the trapdoor again. He kept an eye on it. It stayed closed.

Every now and then he stopped. He listened for sounds, looked for traces of the enemy. He studied the walls. Sometimes the walls were false. They hid tiny rooms. And in the rooms were Viet Cong, waiting. And when the "tunnel rats" least expected it, the "VC" would kick out the wall. Then they would attack with knives, guns, and spears.

Suddenly a huge centipede crawled down Mike's arm. He knocked it away. Then he smashed it with his fist.

"What was that?" groaned Reno.

"Nothin'," said Mike. His voice sounded feeble. Sweat dripped from his forehead. His heart raced. He took a deep breath. Then he began crawling backwards again.

Reno seemed to be getting heavier and

heavier. The tunnel seemed to be getting narrower. It was closing in on him. And suddenly he wanted to scream. The centipede was on his arm again! It was the same one! It began to swell, to grow. It turned into a snake. Mike froze as it kept growing. Then it looped around him. It was crushing him, wrapping itself around his neck and chest. Mike was gagging, gasping for breath. He grabbed at the snake. It wasn't there. It wasn't real. It was only in his head.

"What's happening?" groaned Reno. "What's wrong?"

Mike said nothing. He blinked. Waited for his mind to clear.

The tunnel brightened. Mike's foot hit something. It was a wall. It was the wall of the shaft leading up from the tunnel. He looked up, looked around. He slipped his head out from the loop binding Reno's wrists together. He dragged his friend. He turned him. Then he stood him up. Strong arms reached down from above. Mike

The "tunnel rat" reaches for a helping hand as he exits the tunnel.

boosted his friend out of the tunnel.

"Hey, babes, we ain't got all day," said a black man. "You comin' too, or you gonna stay down there?"

"What?" said Mike. He was staring down the tunnel. He felt confused, lost.

"Come on, dude," said someone else up above.

Mike reached up. Many hands grabbed his hands and arms. He was yanked, pulled. Digging his boots into the side of the shaft, he climbed out into the fresh air. His legs felt wobbly, weak. He sat down heavily. Still gasping for breath, he leaned back against the blasted stump of a tree.

"Well done, soldier," said Lieutenant Knowles. He was smiling broadly.

Mike looked away. "Thanks," he said.

For his courageous act, Mike Lang was awarded the Silver Star. However, he chose to finish his tour of duty topside. Never again did he go down into the tunnels of Cu Chi.

3

FLOOD!

It was the morning of Tuesday, March 25, 1913. Heavy rain pounded down on the Midwest. It had been storming for days. And all the water seemed to be going in the same direction. It all seemed to be headed into the city of Dayton, Ohio.

Mary Althoff was on her way to work. She was the director of the Dayton Public Library. It was only a two-block walk from her house to the library, but she was getting soaked. In some places she had to step through water that was almost up to her knees.

Flood water races through the center of the city. Notice the horses and the water level in relation to the streetlights.

Reaching the library steps, she paused for a moment and gazed out at the city. Through gray sheets of rain she could see the Great Miami River. It was huge and swollen. Yellow-brown water ripped past.

31

It was inches from the top of the levee, the embankment holding back the river. The levee was thirty feet above the city.

Lord help us if the levee goes! thought Mary as she entered the library. She removed her soaked coat and overshoes. Then she went down to the basement. Her two assistants, Ed and Theresa, were already at work there. Water was seeping into the basement. Ed and Theresa were stacking all the books on the higher shelves to protect them.

Mary joined the others in the back-breaking job. After two hours the work was almost done. Mary and Ed went up to the first floor to check the books there. Suddenly they heard a strange and terrible sound. They ran to the window.

"The levee. It's going!" cried Mary.

She and Ed stared in horror. The levee was caving in. A huge wave was roaring through the city. It seemed to be taking the city with it. The wall of water ripped out gates and fences. Trees and poles

The river has risen over 30 feet and is swallowing up a bridge.

crashed down. It slammed into houses. They rocked on their foundations. Some came apart and were swept away. It picked up cars and carts. They bobbed along in the torrent as though they were toys.

"Oh, no!" cried Ed. "Oh, no!"

The monster wave had turned and was headed toward the library. In the next instant there was the sound of breaking glass, followed by a cry for help.

"Theresa!" yelled Mary.

She and Ed headed down to the basement. But already it was too late. Windows were shattering. Huge streams of brown water gushed through the openings. Bookcases were falling everywhere. The water was already halfway to the ceiling—and still rising.

"Theresa!" cried Mary again.

The lights went out. Everything went black. Water was gurgling up the steps.

"She's gone!" said Ed.

Together the two made their way to the first floor. Suddenly the door burst open. A group of drenched people straggled in.

"It's awful," said one man, forcing the door closed. "Awful!"

Water was spreading across the floor. It was coming under the front door and up from the basement.

"Follow me!" yelled Mary, leading the others up to the top floor.

The top floor was a museum. There were glass cases filled with antiques from early America. On the walls were the skins of animals—zebras and buffalo and leopards. From the ceiling hung a large Indian war canoe.

Most of the people slumped down on the floor. Mary and some of the others went to the window. They were happy to see one thing: the water was not rising any higher. But all felt sick inside. A river was sweeping through the city. Floating along on the surface was everything that could be imagined. There were sofas and trees and kettles and gates and parts of houses. But the worst thing was the people. Many people were being carried along too. They clung to boards and other debris. Mary wished there was something she could do for them. She knew there wasn't. All she could do was pray they would all reach high ground safely.

Mary turned to the people in the library. They were all soaking wet. They were shivering and blue with the cold.

Mary pulled the animal skins from the walls. The people wrapped themselves in the skins.

Time passed slowly. Some slept. Suddenly Ed let out a cry. Mary and the others rushed to the window.

"The dam at the reservoir must have gone!" yelled Ed.

Another huge wall of water was rolling over the already drowned city. It slammed into the library. Mary heard the first-floor doors burst open. Then came the sound of bookcases toppling. Books tumbled and splattered into water.

"Don't worry. We're safe up here," she told the others. "It won't get this high."

The water was just a few feet below the second-floor window. Mary stared out at the monstrous river of water hissing through the city.

Ed was pointing. "Look!" he cried.

Mary stared at an unbelievable sight. A whole house was floating past the library! The front door was open. A man and his wife were staring out in terror. They wanted to leave their strange houseboat, but they couldn't. The house continued on its journey. It disappeared from view.

Then they saw something even stranger. There was a young man on a horse. He was riding a swimming horse, a horse carried along in the current! Horse and rider were swept toward the library. Suddenly both became tangled in the branches of a tall tree. The horse was swept away. The young man grabbed onto branches. He saw the faces staring at him from the window. He called for help.

Mary opened the window. "Hang on," she called.

"If only we had a rope," said Ed. "He's too far away."

For many hours the boy clung shivering to the tree. Finally he could stand no more. He made a leap at the window. The current almost carried him away. Mary and the others grabbed him at the last second and pulled him inside. They wrapped him in one of the buffalo robes.

Night came to the flooded city. Those in the library wrapped their animal skins about themselves. They talked in hushed tones. One by one, they drifted off to sleep.

Morning dawned gray and bleak. But it wasn't raining. Better yet, the water level was going down.

"I think the worst is over," said Mary. She was gazing out at the ruined city. She shook her head. She felt like crying.

Behind her, two men were standing on cases. They pulled the old Indian canoe down from the ceiling. They carried it to the window.

"What in the world are you doing?" asked Mary.

"We'll go get help," said one of the men.

The two pushed the canoe out of the window. They lowered themselves into the strange craft. A moment later they were paddling away.

"Godspeed," said Mary.

Everyone watched as they paddled off. The current was still strong. They seemed to be struggling. They fought their way around the corner of a building through debris-filled water. A gray, swirling mist gobbled them from view.

"They haven't got a chance," said a woman wrapped in a zebra skin. "They'll be killed in that stupid little canoe. They'll never make it."

Mary gave the woman an angry look. "Don't you bet on it," she snapped.

Hours passed. Everyone gave up hope. Everyone except Mary. She stood by the window. She waited, worried sick about those in the funny old canoe. Suddenly she began to cry. Then she laughed with happiness. A rowboat was headed toward the library!

The others ran to the window.

Mary was laughing, waving. She waved at those in the rowboat. And she waved at two men on a far-off bit of high ground. They were too far away to see clearly. But

The worst of the storm is over. Men in a rowboat search for stranded survivors.

Mary knew who they were. On the ground between them was an old Indian canoe.

"They made it!" whooped Ed.

"Yes," said Mary. "They did. *We* did. We were lucky." Her expression saddened. "But all the others?" she asked. "How many others didn't? How many?"

Ed hung his head and looked away.

4

JUNGLE OF DEATH

Leonard Clark was an explorer. He had been to many strange and frightening places. But he had never been to one place. It was called the "jungle of death."

This jungle was in South America, in eastern Peru. A huge river flowed down through it. Many others had tried going down the river through the jungle. All had died. The last man who had tried had been swallowed whole by a giant snake!

Other terrors were in the jungle. There were dozens of dangerous animals. There were millions of insects. Some were deadly. The bite from one type of ant caused blindness. Last but not least, in the river there were fresh-water sharks, electric eels, and piranha. Piranha are fish with razor-sharp teeth. They can eat a human in less than a minute.

But the worst thing was the people of the jungle. Most were cannibals. They ate people. They also cut off their heads. They shrunk the heads down to two to three inches.

With his friends Jorge and José, Clark prepared for a journey into the jungle of death. They would travel light. For the most part they would live off the land. Between the three of them, they had one shotgun, several boxes of shells, a pistol, two knives, a packet of fishhooks, and a machete. A compass, flashlight, camera, and extra clothing rounded out the lot of their supplies.

Finally, all was ready. Wearing leather shirts, homespun pants, and heavy boots, the three set off into the jungle. They found themselves hacking their way through a green world. They pushed their way through spider webs that looked like big nets. Fire ants stung them. Rain poured down on them. They entered one area that was crawling with snakes. There seemed to be thousands of them. The snakes coiled in the branches of trees. They slithered along the wet ground. Some were harmless. Others were deadly.

After many days they reached an Indian village. The Indians were strange. They worshipped snakes. Their teeth were painted black and filed to points. And they hissed. The Indians hissed at Clark and his companions. In every way, they looked and acted like snakes!

Clark bought a canoe from these people. He also hired an Indian to help paddle it. The men set off down the river.

They made good time. The days slid by. Often they stopped to hunt for food. They ate whatever the jungle had to offer. There were different types of fruits and

An Amazon hunter stands in a dugout canoe. The fallen deer at his feet will feed his family for many days.

nuts. They ate frogs, monkeys, turtle eggs, and fat worms. The worms were pulled from rotting trees then cooked over a fire.

As they paddled down the river they often spotted Indians staring out from the jungle at them. When seen, the Indians hissed.

They came to a village and paddled to shore. The people looked cruel and ugly. Their bodies were smeared with oil and painted bright colors. The worst of the bunch was a witch doctor. He wore a robe made of human skin! He hissed through pointed teeth that the explorers would soon die.

Clark and his companions got out of the village as soon as possible. The river began moving faster. Then it became a raging torrent. The men paddled for their lives. Waves six feet high spilled over them. The canoe slammed against a huge rock. Jorge was thrown out and carried away in the current. Clark and the others paddled after him. The river was slowing, and they were almost to Jorge. But a swarm

45

of crocodiles was streaking toward him! Not a second too early, Clark pulled his friend back into the canoe.

They came to a smooth stretch in the river. They paddled toward shore. Gasping for breath, they rested in the canoe. Suddenly an arrow streaked out from the jungle. It hit the Indian Clark had hired to help paddle the canoe. The man went overboard. Hundreds of piranha attacked him.

More arrows smacked into the canoe and whistled overhead. Clark, José, and Jorge paddled for their lives. They headed down the middle of the huge river. They had to keep away from the shore. They had to keep away from where the Indians could get them.

Days passed. They stayed on the river. It was too dangerous to go ashore. In the jungle the Indians were watching, waiting. They were waiting for the explorers to make a mistake, waiting for them to get close enough to attack.

Food, that was their greatest problem. The men in the canoe had none. They could not even fish; the river was running too fast for that. They became thin, skeletal. They were slowly starving. So what if there were savages in the jungle? So what if going ashore meant sudden death? Facing the cannibals head-on was better than a slow death in the middle of a seemingly endless river. They had no choice but to go ashore and find food.

It was night as they paddled the canoe onto a stretch of beach. It seemed deserted. In the moonlight they gathered fruit and nuts. With spears they hunted small animals, frogs, and birds. They loaded the food into their canoe. Then for a moment they sat on the beach and rested and ate some of the fruit. They even spoke of spending the night on the beach. Their muscles ached from being in the cramped, tiny canoe for so long. How nice it would be to be able to stretch out for a good night's sleep!

They were talking in hushed tones when suddenly they froze with fear. Hundreds of cannibals stepped out of the jungle! A huge circle of them closed on Clark and his companions. Clark fired warning shots over their heads. The circle kept closing. He emptied his gun, then threw it down. The situation was hopeless. They had been captured by flesh-eating savages!

Clark and José and Jorge were taken to a village. They were thrown into a shack. It had wooden sides and a grass roof.

"We are dead men," said Jorge. "They are going to eat us!"

Two days passed. Outside, the women and children laughed at them. They slipped snakes in under the floor every now and then to scare the men. The snakes were frightening. But they were also food. They killed the snakes and ate them raw.

"We're going to get out of here," said Clark.

"How?" asked José.

Clark pointed up at the thatched grass roof.

A cannibal woman of the Amazon. Note the snake in the basket, the dead monkey serving as a hat, and the cuts and sores on the woman's hands.

They waited until the middle of the night. Jorge climbed onto Clark's shoulders. Then he grabbed onto a beam and pulled himself up. Standing on the beam he slowly made a hole in the roof. Then he reached down and pulled up Clark and

José. Quietly, the three men crawled through the hole and out onto the roof.

There was a guard below. He was asleep. The three men jumped from the roof. They raced into the jungle. Suddenly there was a yell from behind. They had been spotted!

They ran wildly, gasping for breath. They had a head start, but not much. Forty or fifty of the cannibals were close behind. They were hissing and screeching and making animal noises.

Clark, José, and Jorge reached the river. They dove in. They let the current carry them downstream. Then they made their way to the opposite shore.

For once, luck was with them. On the beach they found an Indian raft. They pushed it into the river. In minutes they were on their way.

The men were exhausted. They were battered and torn. Their clothes were in shreds. Their bodies were covered with deep scratches and cuts. But their biggest problem was the cannibals. The jungle was still filled with them.

José had an idea. In the dark, they stopped on a large sandbar. They took off their clothes and smeared their bodies with red clay. They tore bright feathers from a dead parrot and put them in their hair. Out of grass and vines they made crude necklaces and bracelets.

When dawn broke, hissing savages looked out from the jungle at the river. All they saw were three more savages—Clark, José, and Jorge! The three men paddled past on their raft. From a distance they looked just like Indians.

For two more days and nights they continued on. They saw no more Indians on the banks. But they were weak and starving and sick. They were covered with insect bites. Many of their cuts were infected. Some had fly eggs and worms in them.

"We are not going to make it," said José. He was so sick he could hardly speak.

Suddenly Clark let out a whoop. "Yes we are!" he laughed.

There was a town ahead!

"It is Atalaya! It is the mission!" cried Jorge.

The men put their arms around each other. With tears in their eyes, they stared at the tiny Peruvian town. Then they looked at the river, snaking back into the "jungle of death." Somehow they had done it. They had gone into a world of death. And unlike all before them, somehow they had come out alive.

5

ATTACKED BY A GRIZZLY

It took over 1,000 stitches to sew Malcolm Aspeslet back together after his battle with the grizzly bear. Most people would have run away. But armed with just a small knife, Malcolm had fought the 750-pound monster. He had fought it, not to save his own life, but that of the girl he loved.

September 30 was the last day of the tourist season in Glacier National Park, Canada. Malcolm, 19 years old, and Barbara Beck worked at a lodge. There was little to do that day. Their boss gave them the afternoon off.

Malcolm and Barbara decided to go for a hike. Hand-in-hand, they set off down a trail. The day was warm and beautiful. Barbara even wore designer boots with high heels—not very good for mountain hiking, but all right for a pleasant walk through the woods.

After an hour or so they came to a creek. Two bear cubs frisked about. Barbara and Malcolm smiled. They watched for a moment. Then they continued down the trail. They knew it was not wise being near the cubs for too long. The mother was probably not far away. If she had the slightest feeling her babies were in danger, she might charge in a fit of rage.

That was exactly what she did. Malcolm and Barbara had gone only a few more steps when a giant gray streak shot from the woods. It was hard to believe that a beast so large could move so fast. Malcolm saw with terror that she was a grizzly, the most dangerous animal in North America. Her silver-tipped fur glis-

A grizzly bear like the one that attacked Barbara and Malcolm.

tened in the sun. Her huge shoulders made a hump along her back.

"Oh, dear Lord!" cried Barbara as the two backed and stumbled away.

The teenagers had no hope of outrunning the bear. This was especially true of Barbara. She was wearing boots with high heels and smooth soles.

Flecks of foam flew from the grizzly's mouth. She bellowed and snarled as she charged. Then she flew at the teenagers.

To protect Barbara, Malcolm threw her to the ground. He twisted away as the bear rushed past. It skidded in a dusty half-circle. Roaring, it turned on him. A monstrous paw swung at him, smashing him in the face. He felt as though he had been hit with a baseball bat. The powerful slap sent him sprawling ten feet off the trail.

For a few seconds Malcolm blacked out. As he came to he heard a crunching noise. It sounded like a dog gnawing on a steak bone. Only, to his horror, he saw that it wasn't a dog and it wasn't a steak bone.

Barbara was lying facedown. The 7-foot, 750-pound bear was on top of her. It was tearing at her arms and shoulders.

Malcolm staggered to his feet. He pulled

a small hunting knife from its sheath. With a yell, he jumped onto the back of the bear. Again and again he plunged the weapon into the fur on the grizzly's neck. The knife was not long enough to do any real harm. It was only long enough to draw blood and enrage the beast. She let out a chilling roar. Then she rolled over on Malcolm, breaking his wrist and knocking the knife from his hand.

Malcolm rose weakly to his feet. The beast snarled. It wrapped monster arms around the boy and crushed him to her chest. It let out an almost human scream. Razor-sharp claws slashed at him. Over and over she tore into Malcolm. She pounded him and ripped at every part of his body.

One blow from the grizzly took off part of his scalp. Another tore off half his nose and sliced his cheek to the bone.

Screaming with pain, Malcolm stumbled backwards. He wiped blood from his face. He grabbed a branch. Dizzily he stabbed at the giant beast, trying to defend himself.

The grizzly slapped the branch from Malcolm's hands. Then it charged again. Snarling and snapping, it threw its entire weight into the boy. The two crashed to the ground in a deadly embrace.

It's all over, Malcolm said to himself as he and his giant foe rolled over and over on the ground. All breath was knocked from his body. He felt a rib break. Huge teeth and claws tore into him. He was in terrible pain. His mind began to spin. For the second time he blacked out.

When he came to, Malcolm was lying on his side. He was almost in the creek that ran along the trail. The bear prowled in a circle about him. Then, strangely, she began covering him with leaves and dirt. Finally, she let out a savage growl and lumbered away, her two cubs trailing behind.

Malcolm pushed and dragged his way out from under the leaves, pine needles, and soil the bear had covered him with.

She was burying me, he said to himself. *She was covering up what's left of me because she thought I was dead.*

He nearly was. His wrist and several ribs were broken. A kneecap was almost torn off. His front teeth were gone. Every part of his body was slashed and broken and bleeding. He could not see out of one eye at all. The lid of the other eye was so raw and sticky that he had to pry it open whenever he blinked.

Even after what he had been through, his first thought was of Barbara. "Are you all right?" he called out.

"Yes," she lied. She crawled over to where he lay. "Oh, Malcolm!" she cried when she saw what the grizzly had done to him.

Malcolm wiped at his bloody face. "Help me," he said.

Barbara was on her feet. "I will," she promised. "Hold on. I'll be back. I'll get help."

Malcolm nodded. He pushed himself up against a tree. Through his one good eye he watched Barbara limp away. Her left leg and arm were bright red with blood. She was headed back up the trail, toward the lodge. He wondered if she had the strength to make it.

Malcolm curled down into a ball. His body shook. For the first time he realized he was near death. He realized how terribly he had been injured. With his good hand he touched his mouth, his missing front teeth. He saw blood pooling under his legs. His head screamed with pain. He tore off a piece of shirt. He pressed it to where the grizzly had torn off a piece of his scalp.

An hour passed. Then another. Malcolm began to give up all hope. Then he heard it. The sweet, whirring music of a helicopter drifted down to his ears. He saw people running toward him. Then faces loomed near. He tried to say something, but no words would come. A strange feeling of happiness settled over him. He felt himself being lifted onto a stretcher. Then he was in the chopper. An engine whined. Out of one eye he watched through an open side door as the chopper rose into the air.

"Hang on," said a faraway voice. "We'll have you at the hospital in no time."

"I'm really messed up," Malcolm managed to say.

"Just hang on. Hang in there," said the same voice.

One thousand stitches and 41 skin grafts later, Malcolm was returned to something like his normal self. The surgery took many months. The pain he suffered was as much mental as physical.

During his treatment Malcolm looked in a mirror. He was very badly scarred. To himself, he looked like a monster. He refused to see Barbara. But she would not be put off. It didn't matter what he did or said. She loved him. She would always be by his side.

"How can you love someone who looks like this?" he kept asking.

"You saved my life," she said. "You're

the greatest person I've ever known. I loved you before. I love you even more now."

Two years later Malcolm Aspeslet and Barbara Beck were married. They presently live in Canada.

6

LIVING WITH THE HOBOES

Ted Conover was a college student. He came from a nice family. He had a bright future ahead of him.

But one day Ted decided he wanted to take a break from college. He wanted to have an adventure. And the adventure he had in mind was an odd one. He wanted to be a hobo.

Hoboes were strange men, interesting men. They wore ragged clothes. They were rough and unwashed. They did what they wanted to, when they wanted to. They "hopped" freight trains and rode around

A hobo

the country. They didn't care where they were going or when they got there. They were free men, happy men. "Kings of the Road," that's what they called themselves.

If Ted was going to be a hobo, he had to dress like one. In a thrift shop he bought pants that were too short and shoes that

64

were too big. And for a few dollars more he bought everything a hobo might need: pots and pans, a sleeping bag, and several out-of-style shirts.

He went down to the railroad yards. In his dirty clothes and with his backpack he hid in weeds all day. Finally a train chugged slowly past. He jumped aboard a freight car. Ted settled back and smiled. He was a hobo! He was riding the rails!

A few minutes later the train stopped. Ted wondered what was happening. He looked out of the car. There was no engine anymore! The train had been left behind in the yard.

Ted felt like a fool. He was supposed to be a hobo. But on his first ride he had gone only a few hundred feet. He tossed his gear out and went back to hiding in the weeds.

Another train came by. It was an automobile carrier. New cars were stacked three levels high. Ted jumped onto the train. He climbed up to the top level. He got into one of the new cars as the train began to gather speed. Towns and cities and fields flashed by. Ted had a grand view of the world. But he felt a little silly. A hobo was supposed to ride on trains—not *in a new car* on top of a train.

In the next few days Ted had all sorts of different rides. He rode in a cattle car, a coal car, and a car stacked almost to the roof with plywood. There was even one train with an empty caboose. In the caboose he had one of his warmest, most pleasant rides.

At long last, Ted was really riding the rails. He was rolling west. And getting there fast. But one thing was wrong, very wrong. He was alone. In his many days on the trains, he hadn't met a single hobo. Where were they? Ted began to worry. He began to wonder if hoboes were something he had just read about in history books. Maybe there weren't any more of them. Except him. And he was just a fake.

Then it happened. Ted spotted a rolling

The hobo attempts to board a freight train.

boxcar. He tossed his gear in through the open siding and climbed in after it. He looked around. A hobo sat in a corner!

Ted was a little afraid of the man. Maybe he had a knife or a gun. Maybe he was dangerous. But something frightened Ted even more. He was afraid the man would see through him. He was afraid he would see that Ted wasn't a real hobo.

The man's name was Lonny. He wasn't dangerous. And he didn't see Ted as anything special or different. To Lonny, Ted was just one more bum riding the rails.

The train rolled on. Ted and Lonny became friends.

In a town in Nebraska Ted and Lonny jumped off the train. Lonny showed Ted a little bit of what it was to be a hobo. Behind a fast-food restaurant Lonny picked through a trash can. He plucked out leftover food. Then he began to eat. The idea of eating out of trash cans made Ted sick. But he did it. To be a hobo, he knew, he would have to do what hoboes do.

That night he and Lonny went to a shelter for the homeless. They showered. They were given some "new" clothes. A tired little man pointed upstairs. It was a room filled with bugs, beds, and unhappy, homeless men.

Ted was having second thoughts. All

One of the shelters for the homeless at which Conover stayed

around him were snoring bums. He was used to a different life. In his world, people fell asleep in their own rooms. Quiet rooms. Clean rooms. But not here. He was in a different world altogether.

The days rolled by. There were other

trains. Other cities. More shelters for the homeless. And more trash cans from which to eat. After a few weeks, Ted and Lonny split up. Lonny had to head north. Ted hopped a train headed west.

The train stopped outside a small town. Ted made his way into town. In a grocery store he bought some milk. He sat down on a street corner to drink it. A man passed by. He took a long look at Ted. He pressed a dollar into Ted's hand. "You okay, son?" asked the man. "Hope this helps you a bit through your hard times."

The man made Ted feel good inside. He had shown how nice people could be. He had shown that people cared.

A few hours later Ted was headed out of town. Crossing a bridge, he saw the other side of human nature. A police car pulled up alongside him. "Get off the road, tramp!" yelled the cop.

"I'm on the sidewalk," said Ted.

"You're smart-mouthin' me, ain't you, boy!" snarled the cop.

He handcuffed Ted. He pushed him into the back of the patrol car. Then he drove him to the local jail.

Behind bars, Ted thought about what it must be like to be truly poor and down-and-out. If he had been clean and wearing decent clothes, no one would have bothered him. But he had been dressed like a bum. And for that reason alone he had been arrested. For that reason alone he was in jail.

The next day Ted appeared before a judge. Ted was going to plead not guilty. After all, he hadn't done anything. But what the judge told him made him think twice. It also angered him greatly. The judge said that if Ted pleaded not guilty a trial date would be set. And unless Ted were bailed out, he would have to spend at least two weeks in jail before his trial would come up. If he pleaded guilty he would be out that very day. His only punishment would be the time he had already served.

Ted swallowed his pride. He pleaded guilty.

Once more he was free, free to be a hobo. Days passed. Weeks passed. Ted found himself slipping deeper and deeper into the hobo world. He swapped stories and shared food and rode the rails with strange men with strange nicknames. There was "Tree." And "BB" and "Pistol Pete." "Tony Baloney" and "The Bondo King." And many, many more.

It was in Montana that Ted saw his first hobo "jungle," a shanty town for homeless men. He had read about them in books. But this one was for real. There were shacks made of everything possible: cardboard, tin, tar paper, wood, and sheets of clear plastic. One was even made of a big piece of carpeting twisted into the form of a tent. Rotting old mattresses served as beds. Smoke twirled up from countless campfires. Sad-looking men sat around them. They talked. They warmed themselves. They cooked their meals. And sometimes they just stared into space.

Ted talked to the men. All of them had stories to tell. Some told of going off to war, then coming home to nothing. Quite a few were running from the law. Many had had families and good jobs. But then things had gone bad for them. They had quit their jobs or been fired. Then they had left their families. They were ashamed of themselves. They were ashamed of the lives they were leading. But there was no going back. That was how they saw it. There was no way back. Until the day they died, they would be bums.

One morning Ted woke up to find he had been robbed. During the night someone had gone through his pack. Just about everything of value was gone. Frowning, he gathered together what was left of his gear. He made his way out of the "jungle" and caught a freight headed southwest.

The next morning the train slowed down as it approached a town. Ted jumped off. Then he headed down a dusty side road. Near a river he met up with another group of hoboes camped under a bridge. He was welcomed into the group. A bottle of wine was passed around. In silence, sandwiches of stale bread, lettuce, and mayonnaise were eaten. Suddenly there was laughter and yelling coming from the bridge. A group of teenagers had spotted the hoboes. They called the men names. They threw rocks and bottles at them. A rock knocked one of the men unconscious. "Don't mean nothin'," said one of the men. "We's just tramps. Happens all the time. Bums gets what they deserves."

All along, Ted had been asking himself questions. Why were there hoboes? Who were they? For them, what was life all about? Were they men who just wanted to travel? Men who found happiness in leading a wandering, carefree existence?

It didn't seem so. Hoboes were sad men, empty men. They were men who were forever running away. They were running away from life, running away from themselves. At the same time, they were looking for something, but they didn't know what it was or where to find it.

Ted had had enough. He wanted out. For many weeks he had lived the life of a hobo. And he was sick of it. Now he wanted to change back into the person he had once been.

He hopped a freight train.

He settled down in the car. He was tired and he was about to go to sleep.

A form rose up from a corner of the car. "Ted! That you?" asked a familiar voice.

Ted could hardly believe it. It was Lonny! It was the first hobo he had met on the road.

The two men talked about all that had happened to them. They told stories back and forth as the train clicked and clacked down the rails. Finally, Lonny tired. He dozed off.

Ted looked at the man for a long while. He kept thinking about the one thing that made him and Lonny different. Ted was on his way home. Lonny wasn't. He never could be. He had no home, except the rails. For the rest of his life Lonny would ride them. He was a hobo, a real hobo, a man going nowhere.

7

THE *CASTLE* SINKING

It was the night of September 6, 1934. The bow of the cruise ship *Morro Castle* slashed through waters as black as ink. With 549 passengers and crew aboard, the *Castle* was on the last night of a round-trip cruise from New York to Cuba and back again.

Sixty-three-year-old Carol Ekern was on B deck. She had been restless. Unable to sleep, she had left her cabin and gone for a walk. She stood now at a railing. She looked up at a black, starless sky. She lowered her gaze. There were lights. The coast of New Jersey was dead ahead. The *Morro Castle,* she could see, would be reaching port before dawn.

Carol glanced at her watch: almost 2:00 A.M. She decided to return to her cabin, where her sister Paula was asleep. She headed down metal stairs from B deck to C deck. She reached the landing. As she did, she smelled smoke. Then she stood back as a sailor ran past with a fire extinguisher. Suddenly Carol flew backwards. She screamed. Then she fell heavily as a nearby wall exploded. It came apart in a blast of burning steel and burning glass and twisting flowers of flame. Fire alarms began to shriek all over the ship.

"Help me!" cried one crewman. He was on his knees. His hands were pressed to a burned, blackened face.

"It's out of control!" screamed another crewman. Flames were billowing out of doorways and crawling up walls. The man had a fire hose aimed at the flames. Only a trickle was coming out.

Carol struggled to her feet. "What's happening?" she yelled.

The crewman with the hose coughed. He stared at Carol. "The fire's inside the walls," he said. "It could have been burning for hours. I don't know. Doesn't matter. The whole ship is going!"

Carol was already headed back down to her cabin to find her sister. The deck and hallways were filled with smoke. And they were clogged with screaming and terrified people. Some people were in formal gowns and suits. Others were in pajamas and nightgowns. One man was wearing only his underpants. No one laughed. No one cared. Everyone was far too frightened to care about such things.

"Carol!"

It was Paula. She was wearing a sundress she had bought in Havana. Carol grabbed her sister's hand. Together they made their way to the stern of the ship.

A huge crowd was huddled there in fear. Most of the ship was now in flames. Sick-

The Morro Castle *in flames*

ening black smoke and burning embers spilled down on everything. Even the paint on the ship was burning. Big swatches of paint were catching fire. They were peeling off and flying away like burning birds.

"There aren't any lifeboats!" cried Paula.

"What?" demanded Carol. Her heart was gripped with terror. A few of the lifeboats had gotten away. But the rest were in flames! They hung in their davits, burning like torches. There was no way off the ship!

Carol watched as several people crawled over the rails. Then they jumped. They looked like barnacles peeling off the side of the ship. One after another, they splashed into the sea below.

"Don't jump!" yelled Carol. "The ship's still moving. You'll get sucked down into the propellers!"

Some of the people listened to her. Most didn't. "We'll burn to death!" they cried. They dove into the sea. Then they disappeared forever.

Carol spotted a man who had two life jackets on. "Give me one of those!" she demanded.

The man was in a daze. He did what he was told. He gave Carol the jacket. Carol helped her sister into the jacket.

It was happening slowly. But the ship was coming to a stop. The flames were licking closer. More and more people jumped into the sea. Many had no life jackets. And most were in their clothes. Their heavy clothes were dragging them down.

"They're idiots! They're being killed by just their clothes!" cried Carol. She took off her skirt. Then she kicked off her shoes. "Well, it's now or never," she said. She ducked under a blast of superheated air.

"Take me with you," said a little boy wearing a life jacket. He was looking up wide-eyed at Carol. "You're right about our clothes," he said. He took off his pants and shirt and shoes. He stacked everything neatly on the deck. "My name's

Doug. I think my Mommy is dead."

"I hope not," said Carol. She put her arm around him. "But we have to get off this ship now. Maybe we'll find your mother."

The boy said nothing. He, Carol, and Paula climbed over the rail. The ship shifted direction. A great blast of red and yellow flame billowed over them. A man only a few yards away suddenly lit up like a torch. He jumped out toward the water. The flame hit the water and went out with a hiss.

Carol and Paula and Doug crouched. Then they too jumped. They hit the water like bombs.

The water was icy cold. It was filled with debris. And it was filled with people. Most were in life jackets or hanging onto bobbing trash. They swam in circles, going nowhere. Many stared up at the ship as though the doomed vessel could somehow still save them.

"What do we do?" asked Paula, teeth chattering.

"Well, we can either freeze to death here or swim for shore," said Carol. "Let's go. It can't be more than two or three miles. We'll make it."

"Only Doug and I have life jackets," said Paula. "It's too far."

"Too far? Nonsense," said Carol, already breaststroking toward shore. "It's not far at all."

"Okay," said Paula, forcing a smile. "I hope you're right."

"Right? Of course I'm right!" said Carol.

They began to swim toward distant lights. Fast, at first. Then at a slower pace. They sidestroked. They breaststroked. They did the backstroke and the crawl. Now and then they rested on junk floating in the water. Always, Doug stayed close to Carol. Sometimes he rode on her back. Other times he dog-paddled at her side. And when he was too tired to do more, Carol put her arm around him and pulled him along.

Ahead, the sky was lightening. They

could see the shore. They were almost there. But every last bit of strength was gone from them. They were gasping for breath. Their arms and legs were so cold they could hardly feel them. Carol was puffing for air, pulling Doug by a strap on his life jacket. She happened to look back. Doug had slipped down inside the jacket. His head was under water! He was drowning!

"No!" yelled Carol. She pulled him up and screamed at him. He spat water, cried. She put one arm around him. Then, with the other, she began paddling and splashing toward shore.

"I'm going to die," Doug sobbed.

"Hang on!" Carol ordered.

She continued stroking toward the lights of the Jersey coast. It was almost dawn. And they were so close. They could see the beach clearly. Breakers began lifting them and hurling them forward. Carol yelped. Her foot had hit something solid. It was sand. And then she was walking, being pushed by waves. She pulled Doug around, into her arms.

Dozens of people were rushing through the surf toward them. Most were men. One was a woman. Her right arm and leg were wrapped in bandages. Most of her hair was burned off.

"Dougie! Dougie! You saved my baby!" the woman cried. She took Doug from Carol's arms. "They put me in a lifeboat," said the woman. "They held me down. I was burned." She kissed her son. "Oh, Dougie," she sobbed.

Carol was too weak to say anything. Arm-in-arm with her sister, she slogged up through the lapping surf. A man in rolled-up pants was splashing toward them.

"I'm a reporter," said the man. "I'll bet you people have quite a story to tell."

Carol turned and looked out at the sinking, burning metal carcass of the *Morro Castle*. She looked at Paula and Doug and his mother. Then she looked

*Rescuers come to the aid of survivors who swam to
shore from the burning ship.*

at the reporter. She smiled. "A story?"
she asked.

"Yes," he said, nodding.

"One you wouldn't believe," said Carol.
She sat down on the sand. She hung her
head. "I'm not sure I believe it myself."

8

DEATH LEAP

It was Easter morning, 1987.

The DC-4 transport plane roared down the runway and lifted off into the Arizona sky. On board were 120 skydivers.

Among the divers was Greg Robertson. Robertson, age 35, was a veteran of more than 1,500 jumps. He was also a skydiving teacher. And today he would be keeping an eye on a six-member jump group. Most in the group were not experienced.

Perhaps the most inexperienced was Debbie Williams, a 31-year-old grade-school teacher. Earlier that morning Robertson had seen her having trouble packing her chute. He had gone over and given her a hand.

Now he and Debbie and the rest of the team sat in the airborne DC-4. They talked over the jump they would be making. Then they made last-minute checks of their equipment.

The plane rose higher and higher. It reached 13,500 feet and leveled off. Already some of the other teams were gathering near the open door of the plane. Then one by one they began jumping. There was excitement in their eyes. There was also fear. Regardless, out into the void they jumped. Soon the plane was almost empty.

It came time for Robertson and his group to go. He watched as the others leaped out into space. An instant later he jumped too. He spread his arms and arched his back. He soared like a bird. He drifted above the others, looking down at them.

"Our plan," said Robertson later, "was

Skydivers in a free-falling circle formation

to exit the plane. Then we would link hands and form a free-falling circle. Then we would let go and dive separately. Each person would open his chute at a high, safe altitude. It was to be a very simple, very ordinary dive."

But things began to go wrong, almost from the start.

Robertson was gliding slowly down toward the others. Four had formed a circle. Debbie was to one side of the circle. She was trying to join up with it. Another diver, a man by the name of Alex, was trying to do the same.

Alex turned his body in midair. He stretched out both hands. He shot like Superman into the circle. He hit hard, very hard. As he grabbed a hand, the circle broke. It turned into a line. Still holding hands, the people shot straight downward.

Robertson explained: "It's called 'funneling.' It's very dangerous. The divers are going down in a line at a very fast speed. It's like a rope of stone people, rocketing toward the earth."

One man, whose name was Fitzwater, came free of the group. By arching forward, as if sprawling over a barrel, he rose upward. Meanwhile, below, the others managed to stop their plunge toward the ground. They reformed the circle. Holding hands, they drifted smoothly downward.

High above the floating circle were three people: Robertson, Debbie, and Fitzwater.

And then it happened. Both Debbie and Fitzwater spread their arms. They went into a shallow dive. Both were trying to swoop down to the circle. They wanted to join up again with the others. They were coming in opposite directions, right toward each other. And neither was looking up. Both were looking down, at the circle below.

"They weren't looking at each other," said Robertson. "They didn't see each other at all. They were zooming straight at each other like two human airplanes. I could see what was going to happen. I knew what was going to happen next, but I couldn't stop it."

At 50-miles-per-hour, Debbie and Fitzwater slammed into each other. Debbie took the worst of it. She crashed face-first into Fitzwater's backpack.

"Fitzwater was shaken up," said Robertson later. "I could see that. But I could see he was basically okay. He still had control."

But Debbie, it was clear, was in bad shape. "She was like a rag doll," said the instructor. "Like a rag doll spinning in space. She had been knocked out. She was floating on her back in the air. Then she started to spin. I could see a lot of blood on her face."

The young woman, he knew, was plunging to an awful death. Saving her seemed impossible. But Robertson had to try. "She was only a hundred or so feet below me. And I knew she was going to die," he told reporters later. "She was going to die, and I just couldn't let that happen. I couldn't live with myself if I just let someone die and not do anything. I had to try to get to her somehow."

He turned forward in the air. He stretched out his arms. Then, like an arrow, he shot straight down. In mid-air, he pulled his arms and shoulders back. This slowed him. And now he was gliding. He was just a few feet above Debbie.

She was still on her back. Blood streamed from her face. She was spinning clockwise. The brown Arizona desert loomed larger and larger below.

Above her, and a little to one side, Robertson reached out. But Debbie was still just inches out of reach. And the ground was rushing up. Robertson knew that he and the young woman were just moments away from a terrible death.

Said Robertson: "I either had to try to save her and myself or save just myself. I had to do something right then. There was no more time. None at all."

He straightened his legs and drifted alongside her. With his left hand he grabbed her chest harness. This stopped her from spinning. With his right hand

94

The chute pops open.

he found the ripcord. He yanked it. Her chute billowed open!

"The ground was then so close I could almost feel it," said Robertson. "I popped my own chute. A few seconds later I hit the desert. It was a hard landing, but I wasn't hurt."

Debbie was still out cold. Hanging limp in her parachute harness, she landed in a heap. From a nearby campground people ran to her aid. Within fifteen minutes a helicopter was whisking her away to the nearest hospital.

"Her injuries," said one doctor, "were like those of a driver who has hit a brick wall at 40 miles an hour. A fractured skull. Nine broken ribs. A bruised lung, kidney, and liver. But she'll be okay. She's a tough one. A real fighter."

Debbie remembers nothing of what happened after she smashed into the other skydiver. "All I know is what I've been told. And it's the most amazing thing I've ever heard. This brave man, Mr. Robertson, saved me. It is an incredible thing he did. I keep wishing I had seen it happen. But I was out cold. I missed the most exciting moment of my life!"

Robertson visited Debbie a number of times while she was recovering in the hospital. They talked about the dive. They talked about what had gone wrong. Again and again they went over all that had happened.

On one of his visits Robertson asked a difficult question. "Are you going to skydive again?" he asked. "I think you should, Debbie. I really do. For your sake."

"No," she said.

"No?" asked Robertson.

Debbie shook her head. "Don't get me wrong. It's a great sport, but I guess I've lost interest." She shook her head again and laughed. "I'm tired of it. I'm afraid I need something a little more exciting."

9

WHILE OTHERS DIED

When 16-year-old Kim Hue was brought to the hospital in the Philippines she was very sick. She was bone-thin from starvation. Her eyes were sunken. Her hollow cheeks made her teeth show.

Slowly she got better. As she did, she told the story of what had happened to her. The story was both sad and terrifying.

It had begun several years before, in 1975. In that year the Vietnam War ended. The Communists overran Vietnam in the south. They set up a new government.

Times were bad for Kim and her family. There was little food, medicine, or other necessities. There was even less freedom. Kim's father decided they would escape. He paid the captain of a fishing boat $2,000 to get his family out of Vietnam.

On a September night in 1978, Kim and her three brothers and her parents made their way through the jungle and down to the coast. Kim and her brother Trung climbed aboard a dirty, smelly fishing boat. It was already packed with people.

Suddenly there was shooting in the jungle. The captain rammed the boat into gear. It plowed off through the dark water. Kim screamed. Many people were being left behind. Among those still on shore were her other two brothers and her parents!

For several days they traveled slowly across the sea. Kim and Trung were heartsick and afraid. They had lost their parents and brothers, and they had no idea of where they were going.

There were more than thirty other people on the boat. All were miserable. Most were seasick. There was not enough food or water. The one toilet was broken.

Things only got worse.

One morning a fast-moving boat with a cannon in the bow raced after them. "Pirates! Pirates!" yelled the captain.

It was impossible to escape. The pirate boat roared up alongside. Cruel-looking men with guns boarded the fishing boat. They kicked and beat the people. They robbed them of their money and food. Laughing, the pirates returned to their boat, then sped away.

The situation was now hopeless. The captain headed the boat toward shore, back toward Vietnam. But then a storm hit. Rain poured down. Huge waves pounded the boat and tossed it around like a toy. Its engine quit. The storm raged for two days. It drove the boat farther and farther out to sea.

Finally the sea was calm. The people bailed out the leaky boat. The captain and

Vietnamese "boat people" battle for their lives against a cruel sea.

101

some of the others worked to try to fix the engine. But it seemed hopeless. The engine wouldn't start.

For days they drifted. The broiling sun beat down. There was no food and very little water. Kim and Trung and the others began to give up hope. They sat in silence, sick and slowly dying of hunger and thirst.

Then one morning Kim awoke to hear everyone shouting and yelling happily. People were pointing and waving. In the distance, in the morning fog, there were several large ships! And the current was carrying the little fishing boat right to them.

"We're saved!" yelled Kim. She and her brother hugged.

Slowly the little boat drifted toward the ships. The morning fog began to lift. A tiny island became visible. The ships came clearly into view. The people stopped waving. The smiles disappeared from their faces. There was something wrong with

A wrecked ship offers little hope.

the ships, something terribly wrong. They were nothing but rusting hulks. All were wrecked and half underwater. Huge holes had been torn in their bottoms by the reefs in the shallow water around the island.

That afternoon the fishing boat grounded on a sandbar. Kim and Trung and the others waded ashore.

There was no plant or animal life on the island. It was nothing but an empty stretch of sand and rock. There wasn't a drop of fresh water.

The people spent the first few days on the island itself. Soon they began moving into one of the rusting, wrecked ships. They made homes for themselves in the cabins and on the decks. At night they slept on rotting, soggy mattresses and wrapped themselves in dirty blankets.

The biggest problem was water. On the decks of the ships the people set old pots, cups, and cans to catch rainwater. Sometimes in the afternoon it would cloud up and rain a little. The people would lie on their backs with their mouths open to the sky. They would get what water they could that way. Then they would go to the pots and cups and drink what was there.

There was never enough.

104

During the day they hunted for something to eat. They found clams, oysters, and sea snails. Now and then they were lucky enough to spear or net a fish. And more than once they caught a seagull. They ate the food raw. They had no fire.

Days passed. Then weeks. Then months.

The people became weaker and weaker. There was so little food, and much of what they ate made them ill. But it was thirst that was killing them. Days would pass without a drop of water.

One by one, the people began to die. One of these was Trung. Kim held her brother in her arms as he died in his sleep. She cried, but no tears came. "There was not enough water left even for tears," she would say later.

After months on the island, only seven people were still alive. They decided to move to another, larger ship. There was a huge black ship stuck on a coral reef. Because it was so big, the people believed, there was a better chance of being spotted and rescued.

The seven began wading through the shallow water to the black ship. The tide got higher and higher. Wind began to howl. The group turned back. Only Kim and four others made it back to their ship. The others were swept out to sea.

The five survivors lost all hope. The days passed emptily, dreamily. Most of the time the people sat and stared or they slept. To move about, they could only crawl on their hands and knees.

Finally, only Kim was left. She was all alone. There was nothing but a terrible silence.

One afternoon it rained. Kim lay on her back, her mouth open. Suddenly she heard the sound of an engine. She sat up. She blinked her eyes. A bright blue fishing boat was passing by!

"Please!" cried Kim. "Please help me!" She pulled herself to her feet. She waved an old white shirt.

The faces of these young refugees tell unspoken stories of pain and suffering.

107

As though in a dream, Kim saw one of the fishermen wave back. The boat turned around. Dizzy, Kim sank to her knees. Then she fainted.

When she awoke she was in the hospital. The doctors did not think she would live. But she did. She survived one of the most amazing and terrible ordeals ever recorded.

And that is not the end of the story.

Today Kim lives in the United States. And she is not alone. She lives with her parents and her two brothers! Caring people heard of her story. They worked hard on her behalf. It took over two years. Finally they were able to bring Kim and her family back together.

INDEX

Don L. Wulffson teaches English, creative writing, and remedial reading at San Fernando High School in California. The response to his *Incredible True Adventures* led to this second volume of stories. He is also the author of *The Upside-Down Ship*, *The Invention of Ordinary Things*, *How Sports Came to Be*, and *Point-Blank*, as well as educational programs and more than 300 stories, poems, and plays, both adult and juvenile.

Mr. Wulffson is a graduate of UCLA and lives with his wife and two daughters in Northridge, California.